Setting- The characters are on a plane, taking a business trip to Australia, when the plane crashes in the Sahara desert. They are stranded in the desert.

Characters

Pilot(Richard Henson)- older gentleman, hair not yet gray, but children are grown. He has a past in the army. Soft spoken unless he needs to take charge. He tends to be gruff but really is a softy on the inside.

Co-Pilot(Male or female)-Younger, still a bit cocky. He/She isn't a full pilot yet still just a few weeks till he/she gets her license.

Flight Attendant 1 - Young woman whom is very snarky, and a poor attitude.

Flight Attendant 2(Nia)- young mother calm and collected very considerate. Very bubbly but not airheady

Alise- business woman, came from a bad home, very tough and sarcastic. She is very active very intelligent but very pessimistic. Grew up in a small town in the middle of no-where

Liza- Business woman, timid, just got hired in. Very ditzy and naive. Just out of college. Has lived in the city, came from an affluent family

Brian- He is the Boss. Proud and narcissistic. He believes women have no place other than being a housewife. His daughter just passed away due to sids. His wife filed for divorce.

Robert- Brian's brother, not in the same business as Brian. He was invited by his brother. He's there to act as Brian's rock as he grieves. He is a therapist.

Hallucinations- 5

Rescue team 4- can be the same actors as the hallucinations.

Act One

Scene 1
Setting- Brian calls Robert

Robert- *(Hears his phone ringing and answers it)* "Hello, Robert Bellont, speaking"

Brian-*(sighing)* "Robert can we talk"

Robert-(*pauses as if thinking)* "Seeing as you haven't spoken to me or our mother for the last few years, I can't imagine what you have to say"

Brian- "Uhhh look I need your help, My wi...."

Robert(*snarls)* "You need my help, after all this time YOU need MY help. Well what did you do this time. Anger the wrong person or accuse them of falsities."

Brian- *(Yells)* "My baby, my beautiful baby girl is dead!"

Robert- "Look, you have one shot, make this good. I never met my niece. Never met my sister-in-law. I'm being the brother you should have been"

Brian- "Okay, little Amelia died of sids. There's no one else to blame so my wife blamed me. She's filed for divorce. I can't do this. Look come with me on my business trip. It gets you out of your hermit cave and I could use my brother. I am sorry. It wasn't mom's fault that dad died."

Robert- "Okay.... Okay but on one condition. We sort out our past and move on. After this trip you WILL talk to mom, understood."

Brian- "Understood.... Thank you"

Robert- "Look no one is perfect, least of all you. Don't try to be. You've at least grown enough to learn to ask for help."

Brian- "Yeah...." *(pauses)* "I'll see you tomorrow then, seven A.M. sharp. Don't be late."

(They hang up after Robert scoffing at his brother)

-(close curtains)-

Scene 2

Setting- At the airport. Robert received a text from Brian to meet them there and bring his own info but everything else is taken care of. They are on the airplane getting situated. Robert is talking to an older woman whom obviously works for his brother.

Brian-*(sneers and turns to his brother)* "I see you've met Alise. She'll be taking care of your stuff and if you need anything talk to her. It's the least she can do."

Robert*(looks to his brother rigidly)* "Look I don't know about you, but I know our mother didn't teach you to act like that. Maybe when you think over what you said and why it was wrong, I will talk to you."

Alise-*(chuckles softly)*- "First I've ever heard someone talk like that to him. You his brother?"

Robert- "I always talk to him that way when he's being a jerk. We swore mom and dad raised him right, but he's always been troubled."-*(sighs and softly speaks)*- "Last night was the first time in five years that we spoke. His wife is leaving him and his baby died."

Alise-*(shocked, cocks her head to the side slightly in confusion.)*- "I didn't know he had a family, just thought he was a real life Scrooge. Don't tell him I said that, he'd fire me."

Liza-(smiles and rather loudly speaks) "Hey, you must be Mr. Bellot's brother. I'm Liza Grace Owens. First, middle and last, in that order. You can talk to me, we could be best friends. -(shrieks)- We could go shopping when we land. It'll be fun, you know after all this boring work stuff that we gotta do.-(speaks faster)- Or we could go to the pool in the hotel. Ohhh how about we go to that fancy restaurant on the beach that the hotel is next to. Or we could go….."

Alise-*(growls)*- "Or you could sit there and be quiet and let the man decide what he wants to do. Besides this isn't trip for pleasure, it's a business trip! You know the kind you have to work during."

Liza-*(whining)*- "Awwwwww working isn't fun. Why do we have to work"

Alise-*(groans)*- "Working earns you money, and with money you can do stuff. You get fired, you can say goodbye to your money. Now sit there look forward and be quiet. We can't take any more of your annoying babbling."

Liza-*(huffs)*- "Well you aren't very nice."

Alise "You're right, I'm not nice, best get used to it.

Robert "Is she *always* like this???"

Alise- "Best invest in a pair of headphones, if you know what's good for you."

Robert- "I'll see to it right away."

(The plane shakes as it hit turbulence. Liza screams as the plane rocks back and forth. It shudders and they can feel it descending. Alise prays before it too becomes screaming.)

Flight Attendant 1- "Please fasten your seatbelts and remain calm."

(They screaming is in earnest louder than before, panicking. There's the undeniable crunch of the plane hitting ground.)

(Shouting and goans. Someone calls if anyone is alive. Someone shouts out for help.)

Brian-(yells)- "Robert… Robert…-*(softly now)*- "Don't do this to me please." -*(Finds Robert's unconscious body and cradles him. He's not hurt to badly a few cuts but nothing major. Brian hears something moving.*

Alise-(groans)- "Brian, he'll be alright we gotta see who else survived. Somewhere there has to be medical supplies. All planes are outfitted with them." -(stumbles to her feet. She limps and grasps her arm. Her sleeve is torn.)-

Brian-(doesn't move but clutches Robert closer to him)- "It's all my fault. -(pauses)- "All my fault."

Alise-(kneels by Robert, checking his pulse.)- "His pulse is strong. I don't see any bad injury. We need to get out of here. I ain't leavin without any of y'all. There a way out, see yourself to it. I'll get Liza."

-(Alise turns, shuffles away a bit and comes out with Liza. She is starting to stir.)

Pilot-(Yells)- "Anyone else alive, I heard you."

Flight Attendant 2 (she's crumpled up in an awkward position) -(gasps)- "Please…. don't…. leave me."

Pilot (kneels next to her, she's quite bloody coughing as he body twitches.)- What's your name, little lady. Where are you from?"

Flight Attendant 2-(softly)- "My names Nia and why, why ask. I'm dying anyways."

Pilot-(grimly smiles)- "Ones last thought should be of home and family."

Flight Attendant 2-(grimaces and gasps)- "I have a daughter, she's three…..(inhales loudly) "I'm from a small town. My parents live next door. My baby…. she's a spit-fire. Has flaming red hair and green eyes. She's my everything. Give anything to be with her……. She's turning four in a few day. Tell her….. tell her I'm sorry….. I'm sorry for not coming home. Her daddy loves her, her grandparents too. They will raise her beautifully, tell them I'm sorry….. please"

Pilot-(watches her go still)- "You're going home, I promise."

Co-Pilot-(stirs and sees Flight Attendant 1. He sobs)- "Sir what about her???"

Pilot-(upon seeing her, he knows she's gone. He looks at the Co-Pilot.) "Alright son, we gotta get out of here, grab the emergency kits, I'll get the rations. There's four others outside already. I'll meet you out there. I'm going to take them out so we don't have to see them anymore"

-(Pilot exits with Flight Attendant 1, then comes back for Flight Attendant 2. He comes back and get the rations.)

Pilot- "Well let's go."

Co-Pilot-(grabs the kits out of the safe and follows the Pilot)

-(They join the others outside the carnage. Alise is looking over Robert.)-

Pilot- "You know what you're doing Ma'am."

Alise-(scoffs)- "I was studying pre-med before I changed career choices. I know enough for this.... surgery is different"

Pilot- "So what's the verdict Miss???"

Alise- "Well there's no sign of internal bleeding, you'd see massive contusions that'd steadily get worse. He's got a few scrapes nothing that won't heal. He's just out, probably has a concussion. When he wakes I'll look over him again."

Brian- "So he'll be okay???"

Alise- "Yes, he'll be fine. Probably will have a horrid headache once he comes back to the world of the living. Does anyone, have a watch or a non-damaged phone."

-(They all look through their pockets. Brian gives Alise his watch. They don't come up with a phone.)-

Alise- "One of you check Liza. We aren't going anywhere to night, looks as if night is falling anyways. Judging by the sand we're in a desert. It's bound to get cold. Anyone grab what fabric we have left."

Brian- "Why would we need any fabric???"

Pilot- "What little we have we can pile over us, it won't be much but as we can't start a fire right now, we'll need it to keep us warm."

Co-Pilot- "Okay Brian and I will go get what fabric we can."

-(The two exit)

Scene 3

-(Alise is looking over Liza, whom is in the same position Robert in.)-

Pilot- "Both flight attendants are dead. Nia... she had a family, a little girl. That little girl is never going to know her mother. That little girl will always wonder why she died and I lived."

Alise-(shakes her head)- "It wasn't your fault. It happens. It's a risk she and all of us took."

Pilot-(sits on the ground, head down.) "I was the pilot.... It will always be my fault."

Alise- "I'm going to check Liza for a phone, she too is just knocked out, I'm sure by tomorrow she'll be up and ready to shop. -(searches her for a phone)- "Yes!!!! she has one. Looks like it'll work."

Pilot-(cheers)- "We could call for help, and get out of here."

Alise-(Smiles)- "Exactly!" -(tries to turn on the phone, it turns on, then off. She repeats it again with the same results.)- "Dang It!!!! The stupid thing is dead!!!!" -(turns and chucks it off to the side and yells in frustration.)-

Pilot-(falls to the ground, head in his hands.)- "Years of military experience and nothing for how to survive a plane crash."

Alise-(turns to the Pilot) "You were in the military???"

Pilot-(nods)- "Yeah...was in the army. Every first born son in our family joined."

Alise- "Tradition in your family???"

Pilot- "Had a weird family, love them nonetheless."

Alise- "Lost my mom when I was 12. Dad didn't handle it well, started to drink. You can guess how that turned out. I took care of my siblings."

Pilot- "I'm sorry."

Alise-(sneers)- "Don't pity me, I don't need it nor do I want it."

Pilot-(puts his hands up in surrender)- "I don't pity you. I wouldn't do so to such a beautiful young woman."

Alise-(Laughs sarcastically)- "Flattery gets you nowhere old man."
Pilot-(scoffs)- "I'll have you know I am only 41. I am nowhere near..... (pauses and shivers) old."

Alise-(laughs)- "I couldn't tell with the gray hair and all."

Pilot- "My hair is not gray!"

Alise-(looks down at the two unconscious forms and sighs)- "They need to wake up soon."

Pilot-(looks down)- "They should soon. Don't worry, we'll take care of them."

Alise- "With what, what do we have that can help them. If you haven't noticed we were in a plane crash!!!" -(panic finally setting in)-

Pilot- "I know!!! I'm the pilot!!! What we have we can deal with. We'll find a way."

Alise-(softly)- "And if we don't???"

Pilot-(looks at Alise)- "Then we'll die trying to survive."

Alise- "That's better than laying down and awaiting death."

Pilot-(smiles)- "We haven't gave up yet, nor will we. We have twelve bottles of water. We need to conserve what we have. It won't last long hopefully there's civilization close."

Alise-(dejectedly)- "We won't survive long. This is a desert the heat and lack of moisture in the air are only going to dehydrate us faster. The more we move, the more we sweat, the more we sweat, the high chances of us deteriorating faster. We're going to die!!!"

Pilot-(grabs Alise's shoulders and shakes her violently)- "We're not going to die!!!"

-(Robert begins to stir slowly sitting up.)-

Robert-(groans)- "Why do I feel like bull repeatedly ran me over, for eating too much beef?"

Alise-(Kneels by Robert)- "Robert, what do you remember???"

Robert-(confusedly)- "I remember the plane lurching and being thrown against the window and jerked around, remember someone screaming..... But that's it"

Pilot-(Looks at Alise then back at Robert)- "The plane crashed. Your brother...."

Robert-(interrupts the Pilot)- "He survived, he had to.... Where is he???"

Alise-(lays a hand on his shoulder)- "He's alright he's gathering things from the wreckage. I'm more concerned about you. You're head was hit pretty hard. I need you to stay awake for a bit."

Robert- "I want to see my brother, I need to see that he's okay."

Alise- "You need to rest. He'll be back soon, that I promise. None of us are going anywhere, anytime soon."

Robert- "Please…. you…. he's my brother."

Pilot- "I'll go get him, You stay here."

-(Pilot exits)-

Robert- "Thank you. Thank you so much. I've lost him once, I can't again."

Alise-(Hugs him lightly)- " He'll be here shortly."

Robert- "Who did we lose???"

Alise-(Looks away)- "You should focus on getting better."

Robert- "Who did we lose, please tell me."

Alise-(nods)- " We lost both flight attendants."

Robert-(sighs)- "Did they suffer???"

Alise- "The one was gone before we found her. The one, her name was Nia, she died shortly after the pilot found her."

Robert-(looks at Alise)- "Did she have a family?"

Alise- (looks off into the distance)- "She had a little girl."

Robert- (angrily)- "He took her, he killed her!!! He took that girl's mother from her!!!! He did this to us!!!!"

-(Brian enters)-

Brian- "You know well that it wasn't his fault."

Robert-(Yells)- "He killed her! IT'S HIS FAULT!!! You know it!!!"

Brian-(sneers)- "So if a doctor does all he can for his patient, but they die anyways, it's his fault."

Robert- "This is different, why can't you see that, he killed her."

Brian- (smiles sadly)- "She wasn't dad……..”-(pauses)- " Dad died after finding out mom cheated on him. We told you that he died in an accident. He couldn't take the betrayal. Dad left us by his own hand, his own choice. She…. she didn't this was an accident. She didn't die cause she wanted to. She died because it was her time. Mother didn't take care of us….. she had her friends, that little girl has a father, has a family."

Robert-(shocked)- "Why, why not tell me the truth???"

Brian-(Looks down)- "I couldn't hurt you, it was easier to tell you that he died in an accident. But… the pain of lying to you everyday, hurt me. I lashed out and I broke what was left of our family. We're going to get through this. We'll survive. I know we will."

Alise- "Robert, I lost my mom when I was 12. Dad took to drinking. He wouldn't come home for days and he'd come home late at night. I took care of my siblings. Shortly after graduating high school, someone knocked on the door. When I answered I wasn't expecting to be asked if I was related to William Deborne. I ended up going to the morgue. My father laid still and cold. I couldn't think. I thought about my siblings first. I went home. I had to tell them that dad was dead. My brother lashed out in anger, saying he was happy he was gone. My sister, even though he wasn't there, wept for her dad. It's the worst thing telling your 16 year old brother and 12 year old sister that dad was dead. You're brother thought he was protecting you. Could you ask more of him."

-(Everyone looks at Alise)-

Alise-(looks at Liza)- "You know that little, annoying, childlike adult, reminds me of my sister.

Robert- "I'm sorry, but he should have…."

Alise-(interrupts Robert)- "He's your brother, he protected you. You have him. Do not throw him away. You're going to need him here, heck we're going to need everyone who's alive. Now no offense, buck up bud, cause we all could die here. Let's at least spend our last days together without fighting. I don't want my last memories to be this. I know that none of you do. If we went down together, then we're going to die together, not separated in arrogance."

Brian-*(nods)*- "I agree, I want our last memories of being friends, of being together till our end. I remember when robert and I were little, we'd go to pond and try to catch frogs... We'd always end up pushing each other into the water and splashing one another. We'd spend hours there. After we had our fill of swimming we'd sit on the edge of the pond and talk. Robert always had an active imagination, and we'd make up stories. Each one different.

Robert-*(laughs)*- "I remember that. It was always fun."

Brian- "My favorite was about the frog kingdom. He said that all frogs had a king and queen and every other frog would look up to them. But there was a few that despised their king and queen. They plotted and plotted. They were going to take the kingdom from the kind and loving king and queen. One saw what they were doing was wrong so he went to the king and queen and told them the plans of the horrid frogs. The frog shaman, hearing this, created a spell. Those who plotted and held ill will to the king and queen and their family, would be cursed to the ugly muck gray and brown colors of decay, they'd be cursed with abominable bumps and nasty smell to them. From then on the evil frogs were turned to toads. They were shunned and kicked out. But what surprised the king and queen was their son and the king's brother were among the toads. This broke their hearts, and the kingdom of the frogs began to crumble. They lost their power, ability to speak and succumbed to their animalistic instincts. Somewhere, out there, there are frogs that still believe that they can be saved."

-Everyone claps-

Alise- "Well you guys sure can tell stories. Just make sure when I become an aunt that you send me some of those, so I can please the miscreants."

Robert-(laughs)- "You don't have to ask twice they're all yours."

Pilot-(grins)- "Well my life wasn't nearly as much fun but I had my adventures."

Alise- "Well go on, tell us."

Pilot- "Check on Liza first."

-Alise checks on Liza, the girl looks like she's sleeping. Alise shakes her a bit, and sighs in relief as Liza responds and slowly wakes up."

Liza-(Groans)- "What happened???"

Alise-(chuckles)- "Plane crashed, now we're bathing in sand. How do you feel."

Liza- "I hurt, and the floor is soft and I'm bored, and I'm thirsty..... How are you bathing in sand???"

Alise- "The plane crashed. We're stranded in the desert. Oh by the way, do you ever charge your phone?"

Liza- "The plane crashed. How???"

Pilot- "Well it kind of, fell out of the sky. How else would it crash???"

Liza-(shrugs her shoulders)- "Well that's one way."

-(Alise grabs a few bottles of water and hands them out. One to everyone. There's a few left)-

Pilot- "So as I was saying, I had a few adventures in my life. I told Alise that I was in the military before becoming a pilot. When we were deployed this guy and I became best friends. His name is James. He and I were thick as thieves. The others and I, we needed humor, we needed a reason to hold onto hope. As much trouble as we raised, it was harmless. Few minor pranks here and there. James came up with one, we did it. We took a whole bunch of potatoes out of the mess hall. stuck forks into them to be like limbs, then we wrapped tinfoil around them in crappy imitations of dresses and pants. We lined them up in front of our sergeants door. When he tried to leave his room, the potato army stood in his way. They filled the hallway so, it would take him forever to get through. The others watched on and laughed as we began to play with them as if they were dolls. Soon the others joined. The sad thing was, we ate our dolls later that night. We even had a funeral service for them."

Co-Pilot- "Tell us another, sir."

Pilot-(Pauses and then smiles)- "Well there was this one time when James, two others and I, dressed as girls and proceeded to throw apples at people, telling them to pick the fairest of us all. We even got our hands on make-up. Oh James was a fine girl. We named her Jackie. I was named Raven. John was Ellis, and Rick was Pearl. I remember James getting on a table dragging John with him. They danced and sang 'She'll be coming around the mountain.'. We even had glitter. That was fun, dumping glitter on random people."

Co-Pilot- "I had seven other siblings. We weren't all related, but you couldn't tell the difference if you tried. We fought.... all the time. But I remember when my only sister got her first boyfriend. She was 16 and my brothers and I gave him a hard time. He was going to take her to homecoming. He walked into the house expected the one in the dress to be Kayla, but was shocked to find my youngest brother in it. Kayla was in on it though. Ten minutes later she was the one in the dress, prettier than pretty. We send her into the kitchen, once she was gone, we surrounded the guy. He was tall.... taller than me and any of my other brothers. Well my dad decided to come out just then. My dad he was taller than six feet. The guy had to look up to him. My dad told him that if he hurt his little girl that, he'd bury him so deep not even archeologists could find him. Well, he got scared, ran out the front door down the block and right back into his house. My sister came out, yelled at us for scaring her date away. But on the bright sight, she had six boys escorting her to the dance."

Liza- "That must have been fun, how'd she get all those boys so quick???"

Co-Pilot- "We were her brothers, we escorted her to the dance. She just got married a few weeks ago. It was a small wedding, and the guy didn't run away from us."

Liza- "I was supposed to get married."

-Everyone looks at liza-

Robert- "You were supposed to get married???"

Liza-scowls- "I'm not an airhead I promise. My parents arranged it. To them he was the perfect person. He was well off, twice my age, but would support me. I was to be the dutiful housewife. You see how well that went. I wanted to go to college, to do something. I wanted to be a police officer. But to my parents, that work or any work was beneath me. My grandma helped me through college, but I never touched my money until after. I have to pay grandma back, but I wanted to live like a normal college student. I figured that law enforcement wasn't working for me so I went into business."

Brian- "Your parents were rich???"

Liza- "Yep, I learned how to play the piano, cello, violin, and clarinet by time I was ten. After I turned 13 my parents quit being there for me. The driver would take me to school, the servants would pack my lunches, make sure i was up and presentable and that my homework was done. There was one maid. Her name was Sophie. She was the mother I never had. She came to all my performances, helped me with boy trouble, braided my hair, took me shopping. She was there, and she loved me. I would play with her kids. I still talk to her."

Alise- "Well that's good. I'm sorry I was so mean to you before."

Liza- "Coming close to death can change things."

Alise- "We might as well get some sleep. I'll take the first watch."

Pilot- "I'll take the second watch. When you get tired, Alise, wake me up."

Alise- "Get some rest."

Scene 4

-(The others lay down close to each other while Alise takes watch. She becomes delirious. She begins to see Hallucinations)-

-The Hallucinations must circle Alise each begin to say something random without interrupting another, they must begin to slowly circle the person as what they say begin to overlap each other and grow louder. One must be her sister one her mother and one her father. They end it by shouting loudly at Alise, Alise begins to shout back. She wakes everyone else. They can't see the hallucinations, But they go and yell at the others and Alise pleads with them to leave the others be. The pilot ends up shaking Alise while yelling at her to "Wake up"-

Pilot- "What in TARNATION was that Alise!?!"

Alise- "They were here, I could see them. I could hear them. Mom and dad, my sister, they were here. Why'd they go."

Liza- She's dehydrated, she's seeing things. This isn't good.

-(Hallucinations of her mother and father stay)-

Brian- "Hey, Alise, how about you go lay down and sleep. We can get it from here."

Alise- "Okay, I think I'm going to go to sleep."

-(The others go still Only Alise and her "Parents" speak)-

Hallucination Mother- " Oh little one, how you've grown. I know I missed out on so much. I love you so much my little tadpole. I'm sorry I had to leave.

Hallucination Father- "I'm so sorry, I'm so sorry, I wasn't the father I should have been. You took care of your siblings when i should have. While I was at the bar, you helped your sister and brother. I don't blame him for not seeing me as his father, for being glad I was gone. You.... You've done so well. Can you forgive a dead old man of his past wrongdoings?"

Alise- "I already have, Dad, I did a long time ago...... Dad.... Mom, why are you here."

Hallucination-Mother- "Because sweetie, while taking care of others, you didn't check yourself for internal injuries. You didn't feel anything, I don't know why, but you have a choice. We'll stay until you decide."

Hallucination-Father- "My little girl, I would have been happy for you no matter if you became a nurse, or went into business like you did. I want what's best for you. I'm here now, I'm sorry I wasn't then."

Hallucination-Mother- "Alise, you don't have to choose right now, take your time. You're father and I aren't leaving till you do."

Alise- "Mom, my siblings need me, but I'm tired so very tired."

Hallucination-Father- "Remember the tire swing I made for you guys. You loved it so much. You played on it every chance you got. When it broke, you were devastated. So you complained that I had to fix it or make a tree house. I told you to choose between the two but you didn't. You didn't get either of them."

Alise- "I remember that. I cried and tried not to talk to you for the longest of time. I only talked to mom and my siblings. After a week you made me chocolate chip pancakes and you apologize but it didn't change anything."

Hallucination-Mother- "If you don't choose you'll stay like this, you'll hear what everyone says, but you won't be able to respond. You'll be in a coma."

Alise-(Pauses as her "Parents" sit on either side of her)- "Momma, they don't need me anymore. I'm being selfish, I know, but I can't do it anymore. I'm tired, I've been empty for years, I've been a shell. I love them but I can't stay where I don't belong."

Hallucination-Mother- "You have a brief time conscious, it's not much and then, then you'll come home."

-(They exit and the others unfreeze)-

Alise-(Gasping)- "Tell.. them... I love them, and not to cry."

Pilot-(Reaches out to Alise and smiles sadly and Liza sniffles. There's a few moments of silence before the Pilot, Brian, Co-Pilot, and Robert picks up her dead body and moves it off to the side. Alise is taken off stage)

(They come back all of them huddling together. They speak of Alice in a short memorial of her)

Pilot- "I didn't know Alise long, but from what I did, I know she's an amazing woman. She's strong, and passionate, smart and caring. She had a rough life, but she lived, she kept going. No matter what she survived. I'm glad she won't suffer anymore."

Robert-(Wipes his eyes) "Alise, she showed me that what I had, I should be happy with, cause it could have been so much worse. She took care Liza and I while we were out of it. Any normal person on wouldn't care so much, we were strangers to her, but she helped us. She kept her pain and injuries silent, as she made sure we were okay. I'll miss the spit fire. But she's in a better place, she doesn't hurt, and she's with her mother and father. I'm glad I knew her as little as I did."

Liza- "I worked with her. We snarked at each other. My airheadedness got to her, but she knew who I was underneath, somehow she always new. She was there for me, even when I annoyed her. She helped me when I was to proud to ask for it. She was like the mother hen of the office. Everything was tidy and neat, things were handed in on time. It was all her. Heck sometimes she would cook breakfast and bring it in for us to eat.I'm glad she has peace now."

Co-Pilot- "I knew her the least, I barely talked to her. But I saw her take charge after the plane went down. I saw her shoulder all the burdens and pains. I saw her try to keep us all happy and not to worried. I saw her pain, even if she didn't feel it or say anything about it. I heard the exhaustion in her voice as she talked about her family. I saw the emptiness and grief in her eyes when she was silent. I'm glad she can rest, and not have to worry anymore.

Brian- "I was the harshest on her. I yelled at her when business went down, and could have cared less if she helped it to boom. I was cruel. I looked down at her for being her, for being kind hearted. I laughed at her pain each year. I didn't know her, I assumed she was weak. I was wrong. She was the most wonderful of people. She was everything a man would love to have, to have at their side. She looked to the sun every morning at the office, she said it was the mark of new hope. While we would complain about snow, she would say, that it was the purging of the past muck in our life, and what was good would bloom again, when it melted. She said it was beautiful, she said without winter, there wouldn't be a balance anymore, and balance is key to life. She knew the meaning of everything. She was an old soul trapped in a place that frowned down upon her. I was one of them. But I now know, nothing is what it seems and we only live once, so why should we live in darkness when we can hold the torches to the night sky and be free."

Pilot- We can't give up hope, we have to move. We owe it to them, to Alise to survive. We owe it to Nia to tell her little girl what happened."

Robert- "We'll grab the stuff. The stars give us ample light."

Pilot- "Judging by the stars north is that way, we'll head north."

Co-pilot- "We're at your heals cap, mush!!!!"

Liza- "We'll tell someone that they are there right???"

Brian- "Of course. We just can't take them with us."

-(curtain closes)

Scene 5

-(Crash wasn't insight anymore, the group is tired. They hear a helicopter)

Pilot- "Here down here!!!!!"

Robert- "They can't hear you!!!"

Liza- "At least he's trying!!!"

Robert- "It's no use!!!! We're just going to die!!!"

Pilot- "We're not going to die!!!"

Robert- "You're the one that put us her, idiot"

Pilot-(Tired, thirsty and weak gets angry and lunges at Robert) "I really DON'T LIKE YOU!!!! We should have just left you!!!"

Brian- "Do not Talk to him like that!!!(Punches the pilot, they get into a fight)

Liza-(Pulls them apart, by then there's no sign of the chopper)- "I don't know what your guys' problem is but I suggest you get off your high horse, and try to get out of here..... Or else I'm going to put you in the sand.

Co-Pilot-(Yells at all of them)- "Don't you see what's going on. We have three bottles of water left. Left all take a drink, we have to ration it though."

Pilot-(Turns to Brian)- "You sure do have a mean punch. Next time, aim for anything but me.... aim... aim for the sand. Thats a good target, beat that up."

Robert- "We have to find someone, a city or something. We're going to die, I feel it"

Liza- "Look, yes the odds are against us. We owe it to Alise."

Brian. "We owe it to our families too. We will make it one way or another."

Pilot- "Let move, we have to keep moving."

Co-Pilot- "We need to rest right now. We're all tired. We'll drop dead out there if we keep going the way we do.

Robert- "Okay we'll rest for a bit how does that sound???"

Liza- "What are we to do??? What's left that we haven't tried."

Pilot- "We'll find a way I promise you that. Don't worry, we'll live, we'll get out of here."

Brian- "What do you mean???"

Pilot- "I'm going off, I can survive. You guys stay together. It's not ideal, but we'll cover more land"

-(Before they can stop him He's ran off. Pilot exits. The other side freezes. Pilot stumbles back to the crash site. He's delirious, The hallucinations come in."

Hallucination 1- "Why'd you come back???

Hallucination 2- "This is all your fault."

Hallucination 3- "How dare you return."

Hallucination 1- "You should have died."

Pilot- "I know.... I know"

-(Pilot is tired and dehydrated, he is weak. he falls against a piece of wreckage, unable to support himself. Alise(Still dead) kneels in front of the Pilot)-

Pilot- "Aren't you dead???"

Alise- "Ohhhh I'm very dead. But you aren't. Now tell me why you came back."

Pilot- "I'm not a captain of a ship, but I'm the pilot of the plane. I'm the pilot of this..... well what's left of this plane."

Alise- "Is that honor, or is it cowardness?"

Pilot- "How is this cowardness???

Alise- "You're were so close, so very close.

Pilot- "Could you ever forgive me???"

Alise- "What do i have to forgive you for???"

Pilot- "I.... I'm the pilot and you..... you died here, and It's all my fault."

Alise- "Don't give up just yet, They'll be here soon I promise."

Pilot- "It's too late for me Alise...."

Alise- "It not too late. Just hold on. I'll be here."

Pilot- "Why, are you here???"

Alise- "You called for me. Maybe now out loud, but you called for me nonetheless."

Pilot- "You'll stay with me, right"

-(The hallucinations slowly exit, leaving Alise and the Pilot)-

Alise- "I'm not leaving you, until they come."

Pilot- "Until who comes???"

Alise- "You'll see."

Pilot- "Alise, my name is Richard."

Alise- "Well, Richard, untill they come, tell me about yourself."

Pilot- "Okay, I was born in a small town. There wasn't many kids that went to my school. My pop taught me to hunt as soon as I could hold a gun. I had a brother, a twin. His name was James."

Alise- "Was it the same James that you were in the military with?"

Pilot- "The very same. He was older than me by a half hour. We never really fought with each other. I guess we were rather attached to one another. Where I went he went. Where he would go, I would follow. We lived on a farm. We had goats, chickens, rabbits, turkeys, and cows. We had two dogs, and four barn cats. My favorite cats were George and Big Kitty. I was little when I named Big Kitty. Ironically he was the runt. Big Kitty would play with our puppy. He'd have to catch the mice for George."

Alise- "George couldn't hunt?"

Pilot- "He was too docile. In the winter, they'd get so cold, so James and I would sneak them inside. We loved the farm. We showed our animals in the local fair. One year, our birds were under quarantine. So for the auction, they had us stand in the arena, with pictures of our birds, we were auctioned off."
Alise- "Sounds like you had fun."

Pilot- "We moved, and that's when I changed. I wasn't free loving anymore. I became harder. After two years we moved again. I was quiet, I had no friends. I couldn't trust anymore. My mother always asked what happened to the good and worthy boy. That kid died. I tried so hard, so hard for their approval. I had good grades, I was intelligent, hard working. I played an instrument, clarinet to be exact.. I was in marching band, I marched on a broken ankle once."

Alise- "And did you get their approval."

Pilot- "I wanted to go into the arts, but it wasn't good enough, I was never good enough. Yeah I had their pride. I was just an object in a glass showcase."

Alise- Ohhh I see. Get some rest. You're going to need it."

Pilot- "Only If you stay."

Alise- "I'm not leaving till they arrive."

-(They Freeze and the other ride comes back)-

Scene 6

Robert- "We just let him leave.... he just ran off"

Liza- "If you saw the direction he was headed in, you would have seen him backtrack, to the plane."

Co-Pilot- "Why would he do that?"

Liza- "He has a score to settle."

Brian- "What does that mean?"

Liza- "It means, he's gone back to confront the ghost, of those he thinks he killed."

Co-Pilot- "We need him."

Liza- "No we don't, he needed something, something we don't know. He's gone to get what he's searching for."

Brian- "We need to move forward."

Co-Pilot- "Which way???"

Liza- "Let's keep heading north."

Robert- "Shhhh...."

Liza- "Are you shushing me??? You definitely didn't shush me."

Robert- "Voices I hear them."

Liza- "You're going crazy!!!"

Robert- "Nooo!!!! They're real!" -(starts to walk forward but Brian grabs him)

Brian-(Holds Robert close to him)- "It's only you that hears them."

-Hallucinations 1-3 enter. They stand behind Brian-

Hallucination 1- "You'll never be found!!!!" -(Cackles)-

Hallucination 2- "You're going to DIE!!!!"

Hallucination 3-(moves to stand behind Robert)- "You're brother doesn't care, they don't care. Come with us."

Brian-(Shakes Robert)- "Hey, hey, what up, talk to me Robert."

Robert-(Shoves himself out of Brian's arms)- "You.... You don't care. We're going to die...."

Hallucination 3- "That's it Robert, yell at him, strike him. You want to, you know you do."

-(Robert shakes his head and staggers backwards)-

Hallucination 2- "Don't listen to them. Listen to me, come with me. I'll lead you to where you want to go." -(Moves closer to Brian)-

Brian- "What the heck is wrong with you Robert?"

Liza- "NO.... this is not good!"

Brian- "No dip Sherlock."

-(The Hallucinations start dancing and twirling around chanting random stuff)-

Liza- "He's hallucinating! They all were. Alise was before she passed. The pilot was before he scrambled back to the graves."

Brian-(As Robert is shouting at the Hallucinations to leave them be.)- "My brother, he's my baby brother. I can't lose him."

Liza- "There's not much we can do to help him anyways"

Brian- "Then we all go back to plane.... to the graves."

Co-Pilot- "That might be the best Idea we've had so far. We ought to all be together"

Liza- "We'll wait for Robert to come out of this episode."

-(The Hallucinations keep dancing for a few more moments and then exit)-

Robert- "They weren't real were they???"

Brian- "No they weren't. Robert we're going back. We decided to all be together."

-(They move to the other side where Alise is waking up the Pilot)

Alise- "They are here, Richard, they have come, but I am to stay."

-(Liza, The Co-Pilot, Brian, and Robert go still at seeing Liza. The Hallucinations enter again, this time there are four of them, each one standing behind one of the five living people)-

-(They frantically begin to ask a barrage of questions)-

Liza- "Aren't you dead??"

Robert- "How are you here?"

Alise- "You all called me, one time or another. I shall not leave till they come."

Co-Pilot- "Till who comes???"

Alise- "Sit, for a bit and rest."

-(they sit but the hallucinations stand in a row closest to the exit but still being able to be seen.)-

Alise- "Let me tell you a story of girl named Tina. She was bull-headed and strong willed. Her grandmother used to always tell her to stay near the house if she was going to play outside. Tina listened to her grandmother, but one day when she was eleven she was curious on why she couldn't stray into the woods. She asked her grandmother why and her grandmother replied: Because wolves as big as cars will eat you, and then I will miss you terribly, and you will be gone. That only made Tina even more curious. So Tina snuck out of the house and into the woods."

Liza-(Interrupts)- "That's not good, she shouldn't have done that!"

Brian-(To Liza)- "Let her tell the story!"

Robert- "Both of you be quiet. I swear you guys are already married."

Alise- "There was no wolves, but day soon turned to night and little Tina got lost. Her grandma grew frantic, and sent some trackers after her. They searched and searched. After three days of blazing heat, and freezing cold rain they found her huddled in the base of a rotten fallen tree. She was alive."

Brian-(Looks at the Pilot, seeing that he hadn't moved yet, or spoke since they arrived.)- "Alise.... is he... is he gone."

Alise- "At least from this world, but no, he is not truly gone."

Liza-(Sniffles)- "Will he be okay?"

Alise- "He already is

-(The sounds of helicopters can be heard, everyone looks to the sky and see nothing, Alise exits)-

Brian- "She's gone.... She promised she wouldn't leave."

Liza- "What, there's nothing. They're gone."

Robert- "What now, we're stranded, no water no food. We're officially screwed."

Co-Pilot- "There's not much we can do. We could use some of the rubble and what not to create a makeshift camp."

Robert- (Interrupts them by weaving his own story)- "Tell our mother, Brian, tell her what I'm about to say.

Brian- "What do you mean Robert?"

Robert- "I mean that a true testament of a mother's love is the ability to see all and to worry about their family even when all is right. It is a mother's job to nurse, to love, to understand and to punish her kids when needed. Most of all to cry when need to cherish life and to mourn when good has left the earth."

Brian- (monologue) -" Watching my parents and the rest of my blessedly large family, I learned what love is. Love is not a mere word nor is it an uncanny useless emotion. Despite our differences and squabbles and yes even many fights we were still united. Many a day, bickering between us sisters were common. My first lesson as a teenager to learn that my mother truly loved me even though I swore up and down that she didn't. I was going through a rough time, I was making myself miserable more so than what was called for. My sister, our baby sister, to be exact had recently left the home and was in placement in a foster care system and transferred to a type of rehab... in a manner of speaking. I was retreating into myself. Day in and day out I would seclude myself from the rest of the world and take comfort in what would only give my mother pain. "

Robert-(Sets up beside Brian, backs to one another. He continues the monologue)- "Now I realize my mother was right about me being a lot like my brother, despite my objections to it. My mother had a tough and rough childhood and despite every mountain she had to climb she made it, I can't begin to thank her enough for all she has been through."

Brian-(takes over then)-"I cut myself that year so much I used everything, things that people would think to be harmless. I beat my locker, I didn't care about anything, my grades slipped. I was dishonoring my family. I became infested with the need to harm myself, to me it wasn't painful, it was pleasurable, it wasn't until months of doing so, did I see the pain in my mothers eyes. She was hard on me, and gentle at the same time, still today I believe she was more hard than anything."

Robert-(Sighs)- " She tried to nurture me to show me the better way, but me being a stubborn hot headed teen ignored it. The sayings still rattle in my mind, what happened to the old you, the nice sweet and enjoyable you. Well sometime back then someone or something had bruised it and then became broken. All the same something withered inside me, it shrivelled up into nothing. I was just an empty shell, I hid from my friends, I hid from my very mother and father."

Brian-(shakes his head)- "My father, a man of very little comforting words, a lack of conversation, a lack of hugs. I craved the attention the light that shined in his eyes whenever he'd speak to my sister. The days where mom had said she'd rather have went away than my sister, still plague me. I love both of them dearly.

Robert- "I have wronged my family, and it's only fair for them to give me the cold shoulder. If I had spoken up and told them how I felt I wouldn't have began to write this. Certainly I am shortening the length of incident but in all due respect I am supposed talking about her. But all I can say as of now for this short little passage is that my mother loved me even when I was fool enough to think she didn't. I do believe I am lucky for having her. I love her and always will, even when I am an jerk"

Liza- "I'm so sorry."

Robert- "We don't need pity Liza."

Co-Pilot- "Tell us something you would like to tell your father, if you could"

Brian- "Why ask that of us."

Liza- "It seems as if you have something to say to him, as well."

Robert- "We might."

Co-Pilot- "Well might as well get it out now. I mean ain't none of us going anywhere.

Robert- "Our dad, he didn't show much affection. He wasn't able to come to many of our games."

Brian- "He didn't really say anything until he had something to say. Which meant we heard little from him."

Co-Pilot- "That must have sucked. My dad was always there. He worked a lot be he always told me he loved me. Heck we even had weird conversations at the oddest of hours.

Robert- "I loved him no matter what."

Brian- "I knew he was proud even if he didn't say anything."

Robert- "Or act like he was. Mother would prod at him. I'm pretty sure she gave him note card on what to say."

Brian- "He just didn't know how to express himself"

Robert- "His father was the same to him, but a bit worse."

Liza- "Must have been harsh."

Robert- "In a way it was but I loved him, we loved him."

Liza- "What happened to your sister."

Brian- "She dug her own grave, and she's currently laying in it."

Robert- "She did a few things to our mother, and to us that we aren't going to forget anytime soon. We might have forgiven her, well at least I have. Honestly I'm not to keen about seeing her anytime soon."

Liza- "But she's your sister."

Brian- "Not after some of the stuff she pulled. Sibling spats are different."

Co-Pilot- "Then what did she do."

Robert- "It's really not worth talking about."

Co-Pilot- "So what about that shelter?"

Brian- (Watches the area away from the group)- "We can do that, but.... wait are those.. are those lights"

Liza-(gasps)- "They are!!!!"

All- (In a chorus) "Here! We're here. This way can you hear us!?!"

(Rescue team is seen swarming them)

www.ingramcontent.com/pod-product-compliance
Ingram Content Group UK Ltd.
Pitfield, Milton Keynes, MK11 3LW, UK
UKHW041901190726
13854UKWH00003B/1008